Angel *in the* Waters

By Regina Doman
with pictures by Ben Hatke

SOPHIA INSTITUTE PRESS® · MANCHESTER · NH

In the beginning,
I was.

I was for a long time.
Then things began to happen.

Inside me, something
was beating fast,
and outside, something
was beating slower.
For a long time,
that was all I knew.

There was something
soft and warm beside me.
Food came from it.

My angel was there.
But I did not know that.

"Who are you?"
I asked my angel.

"You will know," said
my angel. "Eat now."

Then I could hear,
and see.

I saw dark,
and sometimes less dark.

I heard the beating inside me,
and the slow beating outside.

I heard other things, but I
did not know what they were.

"Where am I?"
I asked my angel.

"Mother," said the angel.

Mother was dark
and full of water.

There was room to swim.

There were bumps
on my hands.
They grew
larger and longer.
I could move them.

I put one in my mouth.
It felt good.
I put it there often.

Sometimes it was dark, and
sometimes it was less dark.

I liked the less dark
better than the dark.

Sounds came from there.

Sometimes
something came,
pushing.

I touched it with my hand,
but it always went away.

"What is it?"
I asked my angel.

"That is the other world,"
said the angel.
"Someday you will go there."

"What is the other world like?"
I asked my angel.

"It is not like this world,"
said the angel. "When you
go there, you will find out."

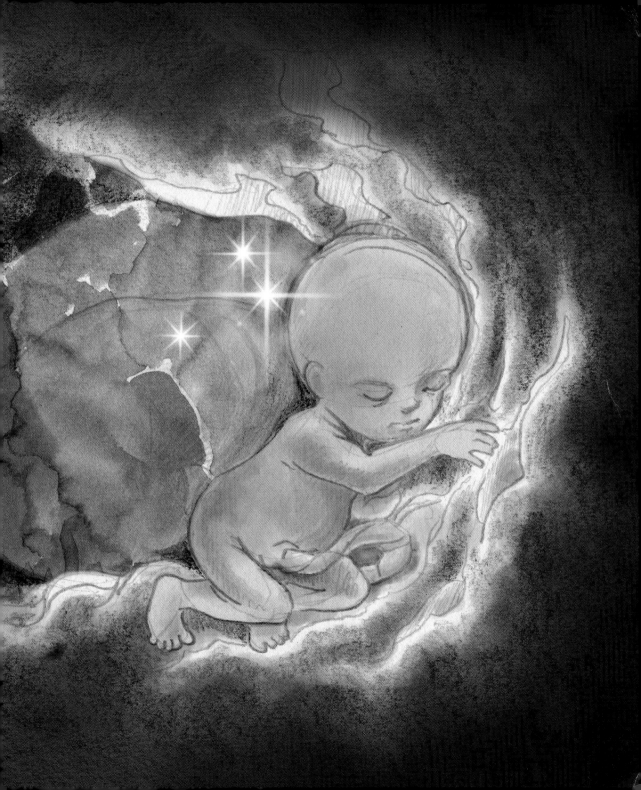

Food always came,
and I ate it.

I slept
with the angel
close to me.

The angel
was always there,
in the dark and warm.

There were sounds I liked
and some sounds
I did not like as well.

I heard more and more.
I listened more and more.

Sometimes things moved, and
sometimes things did not move.

When things did not move, I did.

There was one thing
I did not understand.
Mother got smaller and smaller.

There was a time when I could swim,
and touch Mother only if I wanted to.
But now Mother was everywhere.
It became harder and harder to move.

"What is happening?"
I asked my angel.

"You are growing," said my angel.

But I did not know what
"growing" meant.

I slept and dreamt of swimming.

Then, when I was moving,
I suddenly found
a bit more room.
Room for my head.

It felt odd, but I kept it there.
I did not know why.

"Something
is going to happen,"
I said to my angel.

"That is right," said the angel.

"It is time for you to go soon.
There is not enough room
for you here."

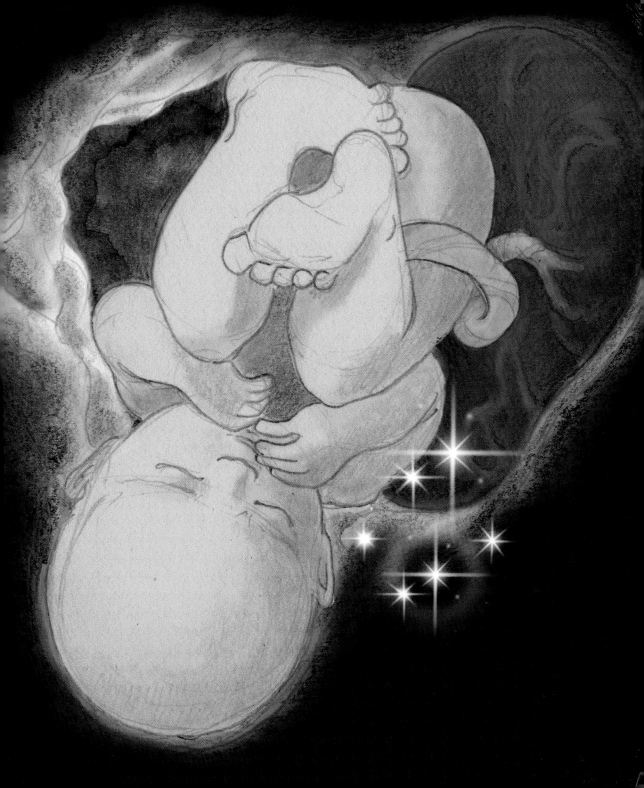

"When I go to the other world,
  where will you be?" I asked my angel.

"I will be there," said the angel.

"I will always be with you.
  You may not see me or hear me.

"In the other world there are
  many things to see and hear,
  but I will always be with you."

I did not want to go to the other
world. But I knew I had to.

For now, I slept.

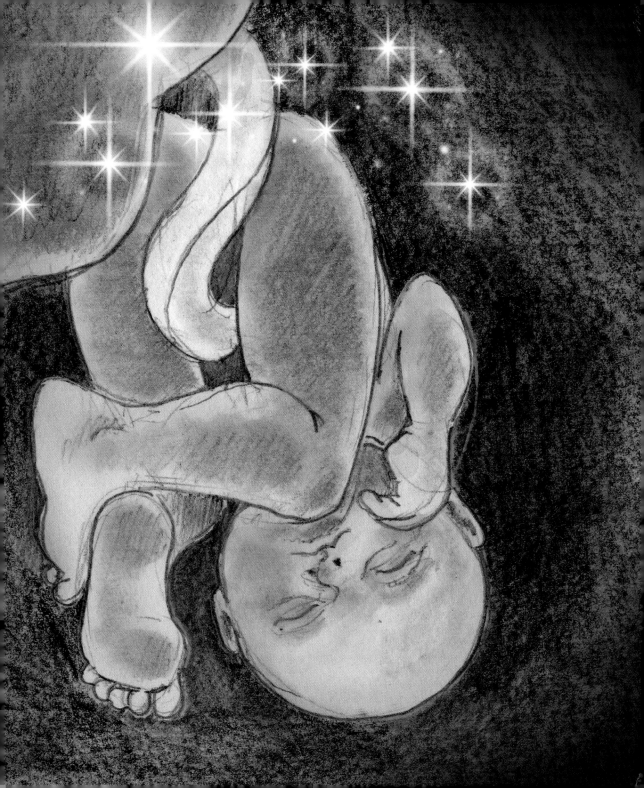

I waited,
with my angel,
and I looked at
the less dark.

"She wants you
to come out,"
the angel said.

"Who?"

"Mother," said the angel.

"But I thought Mother was a place."

"She is more than a place,"
the angel said. "You will find out soon."

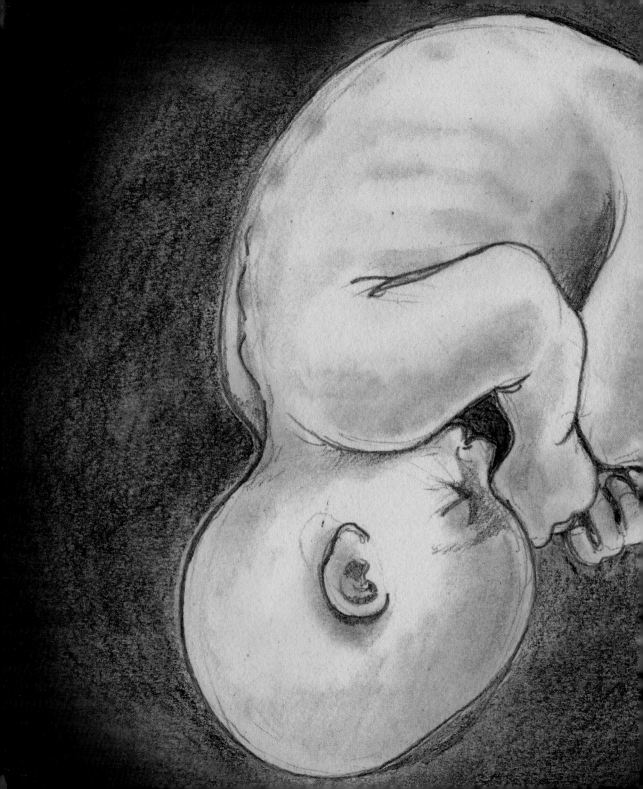

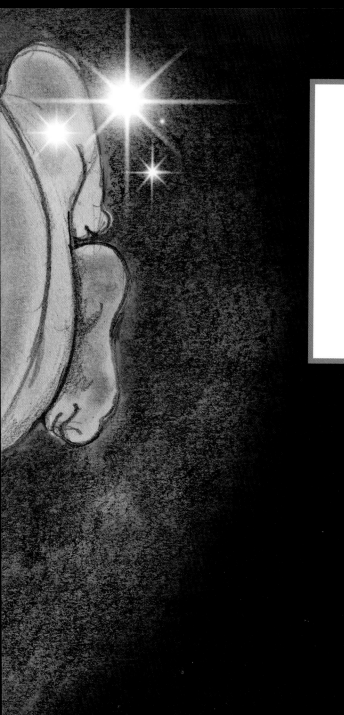

It was dark,
and then less dark.

I needed room
for my head.

I decided to go.

Then everything moved.
Things pushed me. The waters
began to leave. I tried to hold
on to them, but they left.

I was sad, but there was
no room to swim anyway.

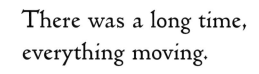

There was a long time,
everything moving.

There were sounds —
sad sounds, loud sounds.

I did not want to move,
but I was moving.

Moving. Moving.

Then there was light.

And nothing else.

No Mother.
No angel.
Nothing.

Sounds came out of me.
Oh!
Loud sounds!

Nothing was anywhere!

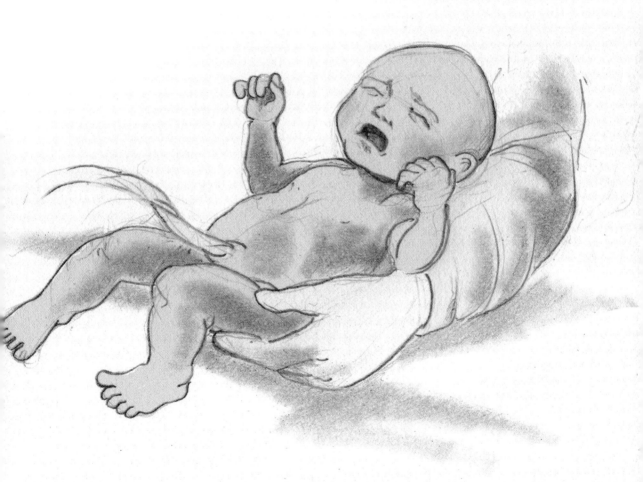

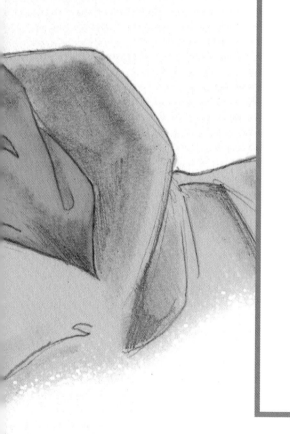

And then
something new
was around me,
warm and soft.

I knew it was Mother,
but different.

I was less cold.
I saw someone.
I was quiet.

It was Mother,
but not all around me.
There were sounds
that were new
and not new.

Then I slept.

I woke up.
I was cold.
I was alone.

Where was my angel?
Oh, where was my angel?

Sounds came out of me.

Mother came.

She was all around me, just about.

I felt warm. Things were better.

But I missed the waters.
I missed my angel.

It was quiet.
All was quiet.

I looked, and saw my angel.

It was not warm.
It was much less dark.
But my angel was there.

"I will always be with you,"
said my angel.

"There are many things
in this world to hear.
There are many things to see.
You will not always hear me.
You will not always see me,
but I will always be here."

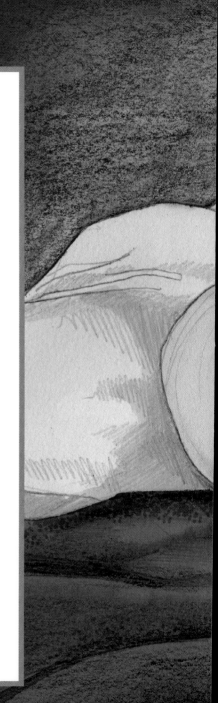

"How will I know you are here?"
I asked.

"When you are quiet,
  you will know," said my angel.

"But I like to see you
and hear you and feel you,"
I said. "I don't like this world.
It is too cold. It is too big."

"It is very big, but you will
grow big. It will feel better
and warmer when you are bigger.
But there is another,
bigger world outside this one.
Someday I will take you there."

"When?" I asked my angel.

"When it is time," said my angel.

It has now been many days
since I left the waters.

There is much to see,
and much to learn.

I like many things.

Sometimes,
when I am in my bath,
I remember the waters,
and swimming.

And my angel
is always there.